One More Step

Sheree Fitch

orca soundings

ORCA BOOK PUBLISHERS

Library and Archives Canada Cataloguing in Publication

Fitch, Sheree
One more step / Sheree Fitch.

(Orca soundings)
ISBN 1-55143-554-3 (bound).--ISBN 1-55143-248-X (pbk.)

I. Title. II. Series.

PS8561.I86O63 2002   jC813'.54   C2002-910693-1

Summary: Fourteen-year-old Julian's parents separated when he was a baby and
he is still angry and hurt. On a road trip with his mother and her new beau, Julian
finds that love—and happiness—come in many forms.

First published in the United States, 2002
Library of Congress Control Number: 2002107490

Orca Book Publishers gratefully acknowledges the support for its publishing
programs provided by the following agencies: the Government of Canada
through the Book Publishing Industry Development Program (BPIDP), the
Canada Council for the Arts, and the British Columbia Arts Council.

Cover design: Christine Toller
Cover photography: Eyewire

Orca Book Publishers
P.O. Box 5626, Stn.B
Victoria, BC   Canada
V8R 6S4

Orca Book Publishers
P.O. Box 468
Custer, WA   USA
98240-0468

Printed and bound in Canada
09 08 07 06 • 5 4 3 2 1

For D. & G. & J. & B.

Chapter One

Purple condoms. My brother got purple condoms in his Christmas stocking. Mom must think things are heating up between Chris and Becca. Not likely. I got a diary.

"She gave me one when I was fourteen too," said Chris. "I used it for about a week. Then I forgot about it."

Mom made a face at him. "Well, don't forget to use the condoms, okay?"

Mom's pretty quick. We laughed. Well, the three of us did. Jean-Paul doesn't understand our sense of humor. Or maybe he doesn't understand period. He's French.

"I learn more English in two day with your mother than I did in one whole year," he said, the first time I met him. I believe it. My mother is, among other things, a non-stop talker.

"Yes," he teased in his broken English. "We get along well. She talk, I listen." I guess it was his idea of a joke. Ha. Ha. I didn't laugh.

They've been going out for about six months. At first, I didn't think it was serious. I was wrong.

"Jean-Paul is coming for Christmas," Mom chirped one morning in early December.

So. This *was* different. My mother gets twisted about tradition and family rituals. This was the first time I ever remember there being an extra on Christmas morning. An invitation like this meant something was up. I wasn't cool with the idea, but I didn't have a say in the matter.

Jean-Paul arrived on Christmas Eve with meat pies, eggnog and presents for all.

"An egghead with eggnog," I whispered to Chris.

"Be cool," said Chris.

"I am." I said.

"Liar," he said.

"Hello, Julian," said Jean-Paul. To Chris.

"Merry Christmas, Chris," he said to me.

"Hell-*oooo*!" I said. "I'm Julian. The tall one. Blond, brown-eyed smart-ass, remember? Chris is the oldest. The short little twerp. Brown hair, blue eyes. The saint. One more time? Me, Julian. Him, Chris."

"Julian!" said my mother.

"*Pardonnez-moi*." said Jean-Paul.

On Christmas morning, there was this real intense moment when Jean-Paul handed Mom a present. She opened it to find a jewelry box. Great, I thought, he is going to propose. But it was a pair of earrings. If my mother was disappointed, she didn't show it.

"They're beautiful," she said. Then she oohed and aahed and kissed Jean-Paul. No tongue, just a peck on the cheek. Thank God. Still, Chris rolled his eyes. I stuck my fingers so far down my throat, I almost gagged for real.

To me, those earrings looked like hunks of banged up metal hanging from her ears.

And they didn't go with the necklace I got her.

Then I found my diary. *The diary is for getting out your innermost feelings,* Mom had written on the inside cover. *To learn to talk to yourself. In the end, you have to make friends with yourself and life will be easier.*

When she says things like that I want to barf. In the end? Like what does this mean? When I'm ready to die?

"It's really so you won't have time to go your bedroom and jack off," whispered Chris.

"What was that?" asked Mom. I swear she has a sonar implant in her ear.

Jean-Paul heard just fine.

"You don't want to know," he said, winking at me.

I guess some things are the same in any language.

My parents divorced when I was a year old. That's always my opening line when I have to write about myself in English class. If nothing else, it'll put the teacher on my side from the start. English is not my best subject. No subject is, for that matter. That line works okay with girls too. They make little mouse-like squeaking sounds. Their eyes turn into puddles of pity. That's all the information I give about that.

First, because it's none of their business. Second, because I don't really know that much. Chris tells me I'm the lucky one.

"That means you don't have any memories, bad or good."

He says he remembers too well a lot of late night angry noises. Not voices. "Just doors slamming and the spin of tires on gravel in the driveway. Mom bawling her eyes out."

He's only ever told me this in the dark when I couldn't see his face. It means he's the one who has a history with our father.

Weekend visits, Christmas and summer vacations. That's what I've had.

So now there's Jean-Paul, another in a line of strange and stranger men my mother's tried out over the years. Sometimes, I think she sees it as taking a new car out for a test run or something.

Okay, so there've only been three. But that's three too many. Plus, Chris gets confused. Four year's difference and he thinks he's a father figure or something. Like I said, too many fathers. And, oh yeah, I almost forgot. There's Poppie, my Granddad, too.

Jean-Paul better not try to do a Dad routine on me, I thought.

"Let's clean up, boys," he said just then.

"Let's not," I said. He just shrugged and gave me this dorky grin.

I turned on the TV and watched him and Chris stuff wrapping paper into garbage bags. Mom went to fry up some partridge meat. Same as always. With fried eggs and cranberry muffins. This year, though, she served the orange juice in wineglasses. Fancy shmancy.

"Who are you trying to impress, Mom?" I asked.

"Cool, cool." said Chris quickly. And gave me *the look*.

It's the look that means *watch your step buster or you'll have to answer to me later*.

Chris and I played Nintendo while they started peeling the vegetables for dinner. It had to be an early dinner because we were leaving for Dad's place. We had to eat there, too.

Strange, I thought. This was the first year Mom didn't complain about how impossible squash is to cut.

"Why are there never any decent knives in this house?" she always whines whenever she's preparing a big meal.

This year, she wasn't complaining about a thing. In fact, she was humming. *It Came Upon a Midnight Clear*. Her favorite.

Chapter Two

Nana and Poppie were coming over for supper. This was a good thing, I figured. Maybe that would mean Mom and Jean-Paul would keep their hands off each other. I saw hickeys on my mother's neck when she was in her bathrobe. She's thirty-seven years old, for crying out loud.

"You better wear your turtleneck for dinner," I told her.

She nearly died when she realized what I was talking about. Then she got in a snit.

"My sexuality is my own affair," she said. No pun intended, I'm sure. I couldn't help smirking.

So let's not see you groping each other in the kitchen while you're peeling vegetables, okay? I wanted to say. I didn't though.

"Ready to go?" asked Jean-Paul, coming into the kitchen just then.

It was time for our traditional drive while the turkey was cooking. We don't go to church but Mom's always insisted we should mark this as a sacred day. Her words, not mine.

For about four years now, ever since we've had a car, we've been driving out to the same spot. It's by the ocean. We go for a walk in the woods and end up on a ledge of rocks overlooking the sea. It's a wicked spot.

This year though, the weather was miserable. It was snowing, a sort of frozen-spit kind of snow. It didn't melt when it hit the ground. Chris and I had to shovel for at least twenty minutes to clear the driveway.

"Want some help? I have a shovel in the trunk of my car." Jean-Paul asked.

I kept my head down.

"Sure," said Chris.

After about ten minutes, Jean-Paul stopped to rest and lit a cigarette. Real good for the lungs, Bud, I thought. "Are you illiterate or just French?" I asked.

"What do you mean?" he asked.

I grabbed the package out of his hands.

"*La cigarette cause le cancer.*" I read.

He laughed, but he only took one puff before he threw it away.

By the time we got the driveway shoveled, the snow had turned to an icy rain, the kind that numbs your face and turns it orange.

Mom came out all spruced up in her snowsuit and funky hat. She had make-up on. The wrinkles under her eyes were gone and those eyes seemed brighter blue than usual. When we started driving, Mom put on the radio.

"Bethlehem was peaceful this Christmas," said the announcer. This made Mom start sniveling. Then she switched the channel partway through the next item. It was about Christmas at a hospice for AIDS victims.

"It's Christmas Day. I don't want to think about this today. Where's the music?"

That's Mom. Get rid of what doesn't make you feel good. *If it adds keep it in, if it subtracts take it out.* It's sort of her mathematical theory of life she explained to me once. Yeah? More like the process of elimination. Like what she's always done with those other wanna-be Dads.

We drove slowly along the icy roads. It gave me time to play the videotape of one of those dudes in my head.

Candidate Numero Uno for Stepfather and Possible Husband was Winslow Thorburn the Third.

The Turd. That's what Chris and I called him. It's all downhill from the moment you're born with a name like that.

Winslow was as stuffed up and puffed up as his name. He was a professor type. Well, he was a professor. A professor of bugs. What's it called? I forget. A bugologist or something. Anyhow, he looked like a bug. A cockroach. His eyebrow hair stuck out like antennae. His eyes were bulgy. I imagined them popping out if he were to ever get surprised. But he never did. Half the time, the guy was in a fog as thick as a cocoon.

Well, there was that one time, the first time we met him. That surprised him all right. Mom announced she had a date.

"Now boys," she said. "Troy is going to babysit. My date is coming at seven. When the doorbell rings, I'll get it and then I'll bring him up to introduce you. I want you to be on your best behavior."

When Dr. Winslow Thorburn the Turd rang the bell, we settled ourselves on the ledge above the stairs. As they walked up, we counted. "One, two, three!" Then we jumped on his back. The two of us. Well, we were only four and eight after all. We knocked him flat against the steps. His glasses flew off his nose.

"Boys! My god. Winslow, are you all right?" my mother gasped.

"Sure," he coughed and sputtered. "Just knocked the wind out of me."

My mother was fuming. Troy, who had

only turned his back on us for a second, was trying not to laugh.

What gets me to this day was that the poor sucker kept coming back for more. We never ambushed him again but we learned, during the two years he hung around, to do other things that got on his nerves. Like squish any bug we could find. Like eating bacon with our fingers and not using a napkin. We just licked the grease off, finger by finger.

"Honestly," he said one morning at breakfast, "can't you two be more civilized?"

"This from a man who prefers the spruce bud worm to humans?" snapped my mother. "And whoever heard of eating bacon with a knife and fork, anyhow? Some food *is* finger food, Winslow."

The Turd stopped coming around after that. Chris and I saw him once, riding a bike in the park. "Julian!" he shouted from across the street. "Chris!"

We ambled over.

"How are you?" he asked.

"Fine, thank you," we said in unison.

"And your mother?"

Just in case he had any ideas about calling her up, I spoke right up.

"She's got a new bo—," Chris elbowed me in the ribs.

"Job," I continued.

"Really?"

"Um, yeah, she's a clown at birthday parties. Loves it."

This was true. *Molly the Clown Inc.* was her latest sideline. Her regular job as a childcare worker never paid enough.

"There's a fortune to be made at birthday parties in this city," she said.

Then she sewed up a costume, painted her face, and studied books on how to make balloon animals. She spent hours learning to juggle and enrolled in mime classes. There wasn't much money to be made, but she had fun.

"A clown?" he said, bulgy eyes bulging.

"Quite a woman, your mother." As he said it, it seemed those eyes filled with thunderclouds. I think the Turd was sad.

"Give her my best," he said. Like a perfect gentleman. Then he biked away from us as fast as he could. We watched until he was a small speck on the bicycle trail. No bigger than a squished cockroach. And that was the last of him.

Chapter Three

I was almost asleep when we got to the sacred spot, as my mother called it. I woke up pretty fast, though. As soon as I stepped out of the car, the wind slapped me in the face.

We slipped and slid down the trail that snaked through the woods. After ten minutes, we finally reached the lookout over the ocean. Our faces were soon glazed with ice—a mix of ocean spray and sleet. Each strand of hair was frozen stiff.

"Me come from Tribe of Icicle People," I said, shivering.

"Me Frosty the Snowman's brother," said Chris, wiping the frost off his eyebrows.

"Now I would like us to hold hands in a circle and listen to the stillness," instructed Mom.

Just then a wave thumped so loud below us, it seemed to me that God himself was mocking her.

"And—?" urged Chris. He was jumping up and down to keep warm.

"And we each have to say a prayer."

"To whom are we praying, Mom?" This was me.

"To the Source," she replied.

"The Sauce?" asked Jean-Paul. "What is this Sauce?"

"No. The Source. S-o-u-r-c-e."

"A spelling lesson, now? Mom!"

"You mean God," said Jean-Paul quietly.

"Mom, this is something you should stick to doing with your goddess girlfriends," I said.

I wanted hot cocoa. Fire. Toasty toes. Mine felt ready to fall off from frostbite.

Her face crumpled. I was sorry I said what I did.

"Can we do it fast?" said Jean-Paul. Then he winked at me. That wink. Again.

"No, forget it," she said. "I guess I'm the only one this means anything to." She pouted like a three-year-old. She's been working with kids for too long.

Chris grabbed my hand and Mom's, and Jean-Paul grabbed her other and mine. Our circle was complete.

"Thank you for my precious sons, for new love and the promise of hope I feel in my heart this day." Mom's voice trembled. Maybe it was just the cold, but I don't think so.

Chris cleared his throat. "Thank you for my family and friends. And please stop the snow."

"Thank you for your presence in my life each day," said Jean-Paul. Heavy duty. "And bless the knitter of my new um ... how you say, glove? I am happy I have them at these minutes." Clever. Mom knit the gloves.

"Thank-you for Mom, Chris, Nana, Poppie, Dad, Erika, Hanna, Maddie and

Luke and the ski vacation I'll be going on this week." I said.

"Amen," said Mom.

"A-woman," I corrected her. We all laughed, even Mom. Then we beat it back to the car. I don't know if Jean-Paul noticed. But he wasn't on my list of people I was thankful for.

Dinner was delicious. Also, a disaster. As always, we ate too much, especially considering we had another meal to go to. But that wasn't the problem. The problem was my manners. The fact that I'm so *immature for my age*. That's a matter of opinion. It's most certainly my Grandmother's opinion. She's been telling me that my whole life, no matter what age I've been.

"Chew with your mouth closed," hissed Nana. I should have done what she said. But, I can't help it sometimes. When people use a certain tone of voice with me, I just want to do exactly the opposite. This was one of those times. I opened my mouth wider and stuck out my tongue, filled with food, at Chris.

So then Nana kicked me under the table. For eating with my mouth open! Kicked me! In the shin! I don't think she meant to do it so hard but she had on those pointy shoes.

"OW!" I yelled.

"What's going on?" demanded my mother.

"Nothing" said Nana.

"Nothing," I said.

"You wouldn't want him to think you're rude," Nana whispered when Jean-Paul got up to get another glass of water from the kitchen.

"No, I wouldn't," I said. Then I burped at precisely the moment Jean-Paul sat back down at the table. I thought Nana was going to die.

"Excuse me," I said. She kicked me again. Harder this time.

"Quit kicking me, Nan!"

"Mom?" said Mom.

Nana's face turned the color of cranberry sauce. She gave my mother a *what are you going to do about this kid* kind of look. I smiled like an angel. Then Chris jabbed me underneath the table with his fork. He gave me the look.

"Frig off," I said.

"Bite me," he whispered. But everyone heard.

Mom looked ready to burst into tears.

"*Chérie*," said Jean-Paul, "this meal is *délicieux*."

"Don't you just love the way he talks?" asked Nana.

My mother nodded. They were chatting about him as if he wasn't even there. Talk about being rude.

Poppie cleared his throat. "After supper, Julian, how about a walk around the block with yer old Poppie? I need to walk off supper before I can try some of that pie."

"Sure, Poppie."

I'd do just about anything Poppie asked. Then again, he never uses that voice with me. Or gives me *the look*. He treats me with respect.

Chapter Four

Poppie's in pretty good shape for an old geezer. Still, his knees are bad and we had to walk slowly.

"Hear it?" he asked.

"I do." I said. It was that far away lonesome whistle of a train in the night. Poppie had been a train conductor for over forty years. It's a job I wouldn't mind doing, I think. Anyhow, he still hears every train for miles around even though he's retired.

His retirement party was really something.

"These here are my sons, Chris and Julian," he said to his buds.

"You mean your grandsons," someone corrected him. They'd all had a bit to drink.

"Well, I guess they are at that," he said. "But I only had girls so these are the sons I never had." Then he squeezed us tight and kissed us on the forehead. In front of everyone.

The thing I like most about Poppie is he seems to understand how I feel without me saying everything. And he says a lot without talking things to death.

"Good day?" he asked.

"I suppose," I said.

"Not used to having another man around, huh?"

"No."

"You've had your mother all to yourself since you were a baby."

"You think I'm jealous, Poppie?"

He shrugged. "Would you look at that place? Lord, what a lighting bill they're gonna have." He pointed to a house up ahead. Even the top of the outdoor gazebo and their birdbath was strung with white lights.

"That's Anna Jenkins's house."

"Girlfriend?"

"I wish."

"Looking forward to the ski trip with your Dad?"

"Totally. It's gonna be awesome. Just Chris, Dad and me. That's a first. I'm taking snowboarding lessons and everything."

"That where they look like they're all on surfboards on the snow? Then they turn ass over kettle in the air?"

"Yep. That's' it."

"Cool, cool," he said.

I laughed until he pushed me into a snow bank and rubbed my face with snow. Then he put me in a headlock. "Listen peckerhead, —you be fair with your mother, hear me good. She's happier than I've seen her for a long time. He seems like an okay guy. Don't forget, she's still my baby girl! Now say uncle."

"Uncle!"

"Louder!"

"Uncle!"

For an old guy, he's pretty darn strong. Even though he joked the whole time, I knew he meant every word he said. I heard every word too.

"I suppose he can't be much worse than Smokey," I mumbled.

"Who the hell was Smokey?" asked Poppie.

"Numero Two," I replied.

"Refresh my memory," said Poppie. "You mean Kirk something or other?"

"Yeah. The guy reminded me of an ape. Nice enough. But when he walked he sort of dipped in the middle. His arms were so long that his knuckles almost scraped the ground."

I did a great imitation. Poppie was wheezing, he was laughing so hard.

"Smokey had chest hair that looked more like fur. It grew all the way up to his neck and out his shirt collar. It grew on his earlobes. Out of his nose. Once, when we went swimming at the Y, I saw this fur also grew on his back.

"I called him Cave Man first time I met him. Chris called him Tarzan. When we learned he was a forest ranger we started calling him Smokey. As in Bear.

"Compared to the bug professor, Smokey was a cheery sort of dude. Almost too cheery. He laughed at everything. All the time. The way chimpanzees do that e-e-e-e o-o-o thing."

"Come on, he wasn't that bad, was he?" asked Poppie.

"Honest, Poppie, he was. And, he smelled. I guess because he was in the woods all the time for his job, he smelled like the outdoors."

"That's a good smell." He took a deep breath to make his point.

"Not a fresh air smell. More … muddy. Like potatoes when you dig them out of the ground. Like rotten leaves. When I asked Chris how Mom could stand the smell, he came right to Smokey's defense and told me Mom was going through a nature phase. You know Chris, Poppie, always the good guy."

"You mother's always loved the outdoors," Poppie said protectively.

"Yeah, but she was going overboard. She even bought hiking boots. Then she got it in her head that we should all go on a camping trip.

"We begged and borrowed camping gear. We planned for two weeks. Mom said it was going to be a bonding time for us all. We even had our bicycles on a rack. Smokey had rigged it up. 'Special for the trip,' he giggled. A whole weekend of his laughing was going to drive me bananas. And that smell? In a tent?

"It was pouring rain the day we set off. Mom was convinced that the sun would be shining by the time we arrived. It was as if she thought she could control the weather."

"I can," interrupted Poppie, "can't you?"

"Poppie!"

"Go on. Go on."

"Well, sure enough, the rain stopped long enough for us to set up. Smokey, for all his years in the forest, didn't even know how to put up the tent. He was only interested in drinking beer while Mom and Chris struggled with the tent. After three beers Smokey was ready to hibernate, but Mom insisted we go for a bike ride. The ride was fun until about halfway through. Then the sky seemed to bloom. Huge flowers of clouds surrounded us. They were the same color as pencil lead when you press tight.

"It didn't rain. It hailed. And the lightening began. The hail hit us like bullets. We looked like we had the measles. Each pellet left teeny red welts all over our bodies. We were wearing our bathing suits.

"Smokey tried to get us to take cover under a tree. During a lightning storm! Mom was not impressed! We rode as if our lives depended on it. The hail had changed to rain before we made it back to camp. Smokey, the last one out of the tent, had forgotten to put down the front flap.

"The tent? Flooded. Our sleeping bags? Soaking, soggy, sopping.

"We spent the night in a cheap hotel room down the road. We ate fried clams and French fries for supper. That meal was the only good thing that came out of the weekend.

"When we asked Mom where Smokey was a week later, she started to cry. Then she laughed. Bizarre. To this day Chris refers to Smokey as the boyfriend who tried to electrocute us all. A forest ranger who instructs you to take shelter under a tree during a lightening storm? Makes you think his brother the chimp had more brains than him. Who could blame Mom for saying good-bye to Smokey? Not me. No way."

"Always wondered what happened to that one," said Poppie, wiping the tears of laughter away. I love making him laugh.

Chapter Five

After dessert, Chris and I packed our bags for Dad's. Mom stood in the doorway like she always does.

"Got clean underwear? Toothbrushes? Gloves? Hats?"

You'd think after thirteen years she'd get used to us leaving every other weekend and Christmas Day. But no.

She has this way of looking all pathetic and orphaned. Except this time Jean-Paul put his arm around her.

Dad came to the door. That was unusual for him.

"Merry Christmas, Molly," he said to my mother. He wasn't looking at her though. He was giving Jean-Paul the once-over.

"Merry Christmas, Dan," she replied. "Dan, Jean-Paul; Jean-Paul, Dan."

They shook hands. My father's a big guy. I saw Jean-Paul wince from his grip.

"Pleased to meet you," said my father. But he was looking at my mother then.

"The *playzhur*, it's all mine." said Jean-Paul.

Chris and I high-tailed it to the jeep. I thought we'd die laughing.

"Next they'll start to butt heads," gasped Chris.

"Bye, Ma! Love ya," we shouted.

"Call me!"

"So what do you think of the frog?" I asked Dad the minute he got back inside the jeep.

"You're racist," snapped Chris.

"Am not! He's a scuba diver, isn't he? So, he's a Frogman? Get it?"

"He's a nice guy, Dad," said Chris. He batted the back of my head.

"Actually, he beat me three times, and I think he's a child molester too."

Dad roared. If Mom were here she'd be giving me a lecture. But she wasn't here so we laughed. Even Chris.

"So, Jules, how's it going?"

I cringed. I knew what would come next. Sure enough. Dad slapped his hand down on my thigh and squeezed. It's his way of showing affection. I know that. But jeez, does he have to pinch so hard?

"Good." I pounded his leg. There, I thought, we have just hugged hello.

"Male bonding is beyond me," my mother would say with sarcasm. *"Men still need to learn how to express their more feminine sides."*

Just as I was hearing her voice, Chris farted. "Ahhh, that felt good," he said. My father burped with his mouth open wide as the Grand Canyon. I sat there and scratched my balls in comfort.

Good thing Mom wasn't in the jeep.

At Dad's place, the kids had already over-dosed on candy canes.

"They're even more hyper than usual," Erika said as we hung up our coats.

"That's a scary thought," said Chris.

"Sure it's safe to come in?" I added.

"Ohh, you two! Merry Christmas," she laughed. She had to stand on tiptoes to kiss our cheeks.

"I'll need a stepladder soon if you two keep growing so fast!"

I know I'm supposed to rag on about my stepmother. As in the wicked stepmother. Erika's wicked all right. As in she rocks! Not that I'd ever want to mess with her. She's Irish. She makes good beef stew and the best pumpkin pie I ever tasted. She makes cute kids too. Even if they are all "yanging orangutans" as Dad calls them.

Here's the photo album of my stepfamily. These are my favorite pictures. I keep them in my head.

Snapshot Number One:

Hanna Melanie Hall. Born April 3, five

years ago. She has white blond hair that looks like cotton candy. Her eyes remind me of wet blueberries. She reads better than I can. Her favorite book of all time is *Go Dog Go*. I've read that to her a bazillion times. When she gets tired she rubs the tip of her nose with her ratty flannel blanket and twirls a piece of her hair. When she's cranky, you do not, I repeat, do not, want to go near her. In this picture she is blowing out candles on her third birthday cake. I'm the guy holding the balloons. Mom gave me that bunch for free.

Snapshot Number Two:

Luke Ferguson Hall. Born September 12, three years ago. Luke would be the runt of the litter if he were a puppy. If he were a puppy, he'd be a miniature poodle. He's got thick, black curls all over this teeny little head. His head still looks too big for his body. His eyes are as enormous as those cartoon characters he's always watching. He drools when he sleeps and he drools when he's awake.

"Shut your mouth Lukie," they're always telling him. So the spit won't run down his chin. Poor kid. No wonder he doesn't talk much.

"We're taking him to a speech therapist," said Erika last month. "We're getting worried."

In this picture Lukie's riding piggyback. I'm the horse.

Snapshot Number Three:

Maddie (Madison) Marie Hall. Born on my birthday, July 26th, this year. Hair sticking up like porcupine quills. Peeling skin with a scrunchy face from all that crying.

"She's colicky," says Dad. "Hasn't slept a night through since she was born. Should have stopped while we were ahead, I guess." Poor Maddie, I suppose she'll grow up hearing that over and over and over again. His line for me goes something like, "I think we had Julian to try and save our marriage. Our last hope." More like hopeless, I guess.

In this picture Maddie's looking into the camera and smiling like a little pumpkin. I'm the one taking her picture. I'm the one who can always make her laugh.

Snapshot Number Four:

Dad. The man I learned to call Dad. He's not my father. I mean, he's my blood father, but it's complicated. I see him with Lukie and the other kids. I watch him with Chris. It's different with me and we both know it. Does he love me? Sure. Do I love him? I guess. Love's not the issue here. But do we like each other?

I think he's a goof. Always spouting off without thinking. He drinks. This pisses me off. "He's a harmless drunk who holds down a good paying job," says Chris. This is true. He's a foreman at the lumberyard. And he doesn't smash the furniture or push Erika around. Still. When I see him drooling like Lukie at the end of the kitchen table, his eyes little slits in his head as he staggers up to bed, I hate him. I hate him for being that ... weak. Big Strong Dan Hall. Not.

Anyhow, in this picture he is wearing a brown checkered shirt. He's asleep on a striped blue sofa. He has sideburns. There's a baby tucked in his arms, fast asleep. The baby is me. This picture is the only proof I have that once upon a time we lived under the same roof. So much for happily ever after.

Chapter Six

The house is a zoo at the best of times. Smells like it too with all those diapers soaking in the bathroom. We bought the baby a box of disposable diapers for Christmas. It's a hint. Yep, there's racket and whining all the time; toys in the middle of every room. Christmas only means more chaos. Even sitting can be dangerous.

"Lego Man just bit me in the butt," Chris said as we settled onto the sofa.

"DID YOU SAY EGGS IN A BOAT WITH A HORSE?"

We both jumped.

"Grammy Hall, sorry! Didn't see you there." She was sitting in a chair in the corner. Hanna had piled a bunch of stuffed toys on top of her. Chris got up and gave her a peck on the cheek.

"Merry Christmas, Grammy."

"SPEAK UP YOUNG MAN! I'M HARD OF HEARING." Actually, she's almost deaf. Also, loopy.

"MERRY CHRISTMAS, GRAMMY!"

"MERRY CHRISTMAS YOURSELF, ALBERT. ARE YOU GOING TO GO TO BINGO TONIGHT?"

"Who's Albert?" I asked Dad as he brought in some potato chips and Coke. I knew his was spiked with rum.

"Who knows?" he shrugged. "Time to open your presents, guys."

Who says having two families is so bad?

"Holy Cow!" said Chris. He had just opened his "big" present. We always got tons of little ones from "Santa" and one big one.

"Look at this, would ya?" It was a 35-millimeter camera. "Cool, cool."

"Julian, open yours now!" Hanna wiggled in beside me. "I helped wrap it!"

"Awesome," I said. It was a camcorder.

"Figured we'd take lots of pictures this week. And we need some of us in action, too." Dad was grinning from ear to ear.

"They costed the very same too," piped in Hanna. "Mommy told Daddy."

After another turkey dinner and another helping of squash which I ate just to be polite, we settled in to watch the basketball game. Dad had taped it for us earlier. After the game everything came unglued.

"Dan!" shouted Erika from the kitchen. "Could you keep Lukie in there with you? I need an extra set of hands in here!"

"Jules, get Lukie!" ordered Dad. That voice. The one that makes me want to say, no frickin' way. But it was Christmas. I had a camcorder. I went into the kitchen just as Erika popped her breast out of her shirt to feed Maddie.

"Oh, Jesus!" I covered my eyes. "Sorry, Erika. Lukie, come on."

When I went back to the living room, Grammy Hall was pointing out the window.

"LIGHTS ARE OUT! LIGHTS ARE OUT! CAN'T PLAY BINGO WITH NO LIGHTS!"

"Relax, Mom," said Dad. But it was true. Half the Christmas tree lights on the tree outside had blown. He couldn't have cared less. It was all he could do to keep his eyes open by that point.

Well, Grammy Hall was *not* a happy camper. She sprang out of her chair like some sort of jack-in-the-box. With her mouth puckered up like an elastic waistband, she shuffled on over to him. Then she biffed him on the ear with a rolled up newspaper. Chris and I almost lost it.

"FIX THE LIGHTS, ALBERT!"

Okay, okay, Ma," he said and stood up. Well, wobbled up is more like it.

"Jules, you stay here with Lukie. Chris, come help me with the damn lights, okay?"

Right. Leave me inside with the crazy woman and the kids.

We watched from the window. I got out the camcorder. It was quite a show.

Dad stumbled around in the snow and almost banged Chris on the head with the ladder. I could see they were arguing about who would go up the ladder and figure out which bulb was burnt out. Dad won.

Chris looked in at me and shook his head.

Big Dan Hall made it up all right. And back down again too.

The toe of his boot caught the top rung of the ladder.

The ladder caught in the tree.

The tree crashed on Dad.

Dad landed on Chris. With the tree and the ladder.

"Daddy go boom boom," said Lukie, the silent one.

"BINGO!" shouted Grammy Ross.

"DADDY" screamed Hanna and burst into tears.

"ERIKA!" I hollered.

Dad was laughing when I got out to see if they were okay. I thought Chris was too. Until he tried to stand up.

"My knee!" he screamed. Tears were streaming down his face.

We spent the rest of the night in the emergency room. Chris had a cast on up to his waist.

The ski trip? It was pretty much down the toilet.

"Harmless drunk, huh?" I said when we finally got to bed.

I waited for him to try and put a positive spin on this.

"Chris?"

"He's an idiot, okay? Just leave me alone."

Then he turned his back to me. And cried like a little boy. I couldn't handle it.

"Chris? I got it all on videotape. Maybe we could send it in to that show? You know, funny home videos? I mean it was pretty funny to watch."

"Yeah. Real hilarious. Ho, ho, ho."

Chapter Seven

"Guess what, Mom?"

I phoned her first thing next morning. I think she was still in bed. With Jean-Paul.

I'm not sure why I phoned. To make her miserable, I guess.

She didn't say anything when I told her the story. "So now, I have to stick around Lego Land for a week. Chris wants us to go anyway but no way, I'm not going without him."

"Let me to talk to Chris," she said. I handed over the phone.

"I'm fine, really, Mom. Fine. Yeah. Yeah. Yeah, he was."

I could hear Mom's voice from where I was standing. Chris winced and held the receiver away from his ear.

"No, Mom. Not a good idea. No. Dad probably wouldn't want to talk to you right now. Mom! No, I won't tell him to eat mud. Calm down." Long pause. "Gee, thanks Mom, but I'll stick around here. Becca's coming to visit today. She'll be a good nurse. Sure, I'll put him back on."

As he handed me the phone back he said, "Hell hath no fury like our mother pissed at our father!"

"Julian?" Her voice was hoarse. "Want to go to Quebec City with us today?"

I stared at Chris.

"Go!" he mouthed. I shrugged.

"I dunno," I said.

"Well, if you did know, what would your answer be?"

"I guess."

"Terrific! We're leaving in an hour. Be ready."

"It's better than sticking around Lego Land," said Chris.

"But you're not coming?"

"Hello!" He pointed to his cast. "A long car trip? No, thanks!"

Telling Dad I was taking off was nasty.

"You're leaving? Just like that?" His face was twisted with anger.

"I'll be bored out of my head if I stay." I didn't look at him.

"We can still go snowmobiling, Jules." He sounded hopeful.

"Every day? I don't think so. Look, Dad, I gotta pack up, okay?" Why didn't he just let it go? Why not take the hint?

"No. It's not okay. You're not going." He used the voice.

"Excuse me?"

"You heard me. I said no."

"You can't tell me what to do!"

"Oh yes I can—I'm your father!"

"Since when?" It slipped out.

"Look at me!" he yelled. I didn't.

46

"Julian, I said look at me." No way would I.

His fist found the wall. He punched a hole right through.

"Way to go," I muttered under my breath.

The house was suddenly stone still.

"This is my week, not your mother's."

"Well, maybe you should have thought of that last night."

"Shit happens, Julian."

"Tell me about it."

"I said you're staying. Stop packing."

"What are you going to do? Make me?" I couldn't resist.

He grabbed the handle of my gym bag. I pulled back.

"Stop it now, you two, stop it!" It was Erika. She was standing in the doorway rocking Maddie back and forth. Maddie's eyes were wide as pie plates.

They were there in the nick of time. I think we were getting ready to punch each other out.

"Sorry," I said to her. "But I'm outta here." I shoved the rest of my clothes into my bag and brushed past all of them. Erika reached out and touched my arm. "Julian," she said. "Your father's been looking forward to this week. Not just to ski. To spend some time. With *you*."

"Yeah, right," I said and thumped downstairs. I threw on my coat and went to wait in the back porch. My heart was pounding. I was fighting back tears. The nerve of that b —.

Chris hobbled into the porch on his crutches. "It's okay," he said, "he'll get over it."

"Shuddup," I said.

"What did I do?" he asked.

"Nothing," I said. "You never do anything wrong. That's the problem. I'm the troublemaker."

"Yeah? So what else is new?"

"Just get outta here, okay?"

"I'm the one who told you to go, remember?" he said.

"I don't want to go, okay? And I don't want to stay here, either!" My teeth were chattering. *I will not cry*, I thought to myself. *I will not cry.*

"The lesser of two evils, huh?" he said quietly.

"Something like that. Some holiday."

"Want to trade places?" he asked and pointed to his leg.

"No way." I made an effort to smile.

"Go back in before Mom gets here," he said.

So I did. Dad was helping Hanna put together a Sesame Street puzzle. He acted as if nothing had happened. Erika was packing me up some goodies for the road. It was a thick turkey sandwich with cranberry sauce and dressing on homemade bread and some sugar cookies.

Truth is, I felt pretty shitty when Mom and Jean-Paul came to pick me up. Lukie cried and said I promised to build a space ship with him. When Dad scooped him up and rocked him I wondered for a second if he'd ever done that to me. Must have. He looked really tired, until he smiled.

"I'll keep the skis waxed for some weekend in January. Okay, Jules?"

"Sure thing. See ya." Erika pecked me on the cheek. Hanna hugged my kneecap. Chris gave me two thumbs-up. Maddie waved bye-bye.

Chapter Eight

It took eight hours to drive to Quebec City. I slept most of the way. Between Edmundston and Riviere du Loup, Jean-Paul played Alanis Morissette on his new CD player.

"Good taste in music," I said. I had to give him that.

"*I got one hand in my pocket and the other one's giving a peace sign*," she sang.

"The other one's picking my nose," I sang. "The other one's scratching my butt."

Mom laughed along with Jean-Paul despite herself.

"What other music you like?" Jean-Paul asked.

"The Bare Naked Ladies are wicked."

"Wicked. This word, you say it all the time. I think it mean something bad."

"It does, usually," said Mom. "It's sort of teenage slang. You know what I mean by slang?"

"Of course. So when Julian says wicked he means awesome, cool?"

"Only even better," I said.

"Ah, *oui*. In French the kids say *écoeurant*. Usually it means disgusting. But when they say it means the ... opposite."

So while he boned up on his English and Mom kept practicing phrases from her French-English dictionary, I went back to sleep. And had a nightmare.

About Number Three. He was swimming underwater. Pulling me down.

Remembering him gives me shivers. A chill in my bones. I've erased his name from memory. But his eyes? Those, I remember. They were the cool white-blue of a killer shark. Reminded me of pictures I'd seen in magazines. The Shark. That'll do.

"He has a Windsurfer and a motor boat," Mom told us after their first date.

"The guy has possibilities," I said.

"What's he do, Mom? Rob banks?" This time it was Chris who was negative. "Greasy," is how he'd described him after they left on that date. "Greasy as an oil slick."

"I'm not sure exactly. Investments or some such. He owns his own company. Something to do with stocks and bonds.

"A con man," she told her girlfriends afterward. Crazy would have been closer to the truth. I don't think she could ever admit her judgement was so poor.

They were hot and heavy for about six months. Then, he invested money for my mother—like she had so much to begin with. We probably would have lost our house if we owned one, but we didn't. We still don't. Probably on account of that jerk. We still rent. All Mom's savings, from her clowning money, were history. That wasn't the worst of it, though.

When she asked him to stop coming around, he didn't.

"He was lurking outside of work today," she whispered to Bette, her best friend.

"He's creepy," said Bette, sipping her tea. "I'm worried."

"He followed me to the grocery store," she hissed into the phone to Poppie.

"Maybe I will," she said. "Yeah, okay, Dad, I'll call the police. That's a good idea."

The police did nothing.

The phone would ring and no one would be there.

Just breathing. We knew who it was.

Well, this went on for about three months. During this time Mom was a bag of nerves. She jumped every time the phone rang. She was always looking over her shoulder. She lost weight. I began biting my fingernails. Chris slept with a baseball bat by his bed.

Then, one night, around two in the morning, there was a banging on the front door.

Mom said after she didn't want to wake the neighbors, so she let him in. Big mistake. He was wired.

"Holy crap, he's high as a kite," said Chris. "Go now. Call the cops."

I crept upstairs and for once did as I was told. It was still too late to stop what happened. The Shark grabbed a fistful of Mom's hair and was screaming at her.

"Bitch!"

"Let her go, asshole," said Chris. Then he whacked him a good one across the back of the neck with the bat. The guy was out cold. There was blood. We were bawling and screaming by the time we heard the sirens. The whole neighborhood was out on the street.

It was nasty. I'd rather not remember. The shark guy was not dead. He charged my brother with assault. Imagine. He left town suddenly, though, and the charges were dropped. Chris figures Poppie and the rest of his pals chased him out of town. That was four years ago. I was ten. My mother hasn't dated since then.

Until now, I mean.

Je suis Molly. Tu es Jean-Paul. Julian est mon fils. When I woke up, Mom was still trying to prepare herself. None of his family spoke English. She was paranoid that they wouldn't like him bringing home an Anglophone.

"Just don't talk, Mom," I teased. "No one will ever know."

"Your mother, not talk?" Jean-Paul winked in the rearview mirror. That frickin' winking of his.

"Something wrong with your eye?" I snapped at him.

Chapter Nine

We took the ferry across the St. Lawrence River from Levi to Quebec City.

"For the romance," sighed my mother. The river was packed with ice. It was like a glacier had exploded. The chunks of ice were a dirty gray. It was hypnotizing, watching them curl away from the bow of the boat.

"Julian, look! It's the Château Frontenac!" My mother was almost jumping for joy.

"Just looks like all the postcards," I said.

"Wet blanket," she said. And stuck out her tongue.

"Time for a bite to heat?" asked Jean-Paul.

"Yeah. I could heat a horse," I replied.

"Okay, Julian, that's enough," said my mother.

Jean-Paul whispered something in her ear.

The café was a hole in the wall. Really, it was this cool cave dug in the side of an old stone wall. It looked like people had been carving their names in the tabletops for centuries. In the middle of each table, straw-covered wine bottles plugged with burning candles made shadows dance on the walls around us.

"Does everyone in Quebec smoke?" I asked. My eyes were stinging.

And everyone was talking French. I couldn't understand the menu until Jean-Paul pointed out it was in English on the opposite page.

"Are you illiterate or just English?" He asked. I biffed him on the side of the head.

"We say *touché* in French." He really wanted to dig it in.

"We say it in English too."

"One more thing the English have taken from the French."

"What's with you two?" My mother was frowning.

"None of your beeswax," I smiled back.

The split pea soup looked gross but it was delicious, I told the waitress. What a knock-out she was.

Mom was staring at me like I was an alien.

"My, we really can be charming at times, can't we?" she jabbed.

"Pretty women can make a guy do many tings!" said Jean-Paul. He caught himself just in time. He didn't wink.

We walked around old Quebec for a while. In front of the Château was the biggest toboggan hill I'd ever seen. Right there, in the middle of the city! Three long tracks of ice humped in places like a water slide, only going straight downhill. The people in those sleds were screaming their heads off.

"Looks like a hell of a good time! What are we waiting for?" This trip suddenly looked like it might be fun. But Jean-Paul said we didn't have time if we wanted to get to where we were going before dark. Mom looked disappointed too.

"But, after all," she hissed to me when she saw the pout I'd put on, "that's not why we came. We came to meet his family. Now smile."

I smiled. For almost a week, I smiled. And smiled. My jaw ached. We made the rounds of nearly all the brothers and sisters. There were ten in all.

We only got a break from all of it the day I went skiing with Mom. Jean-Paul wanted to shop for some new scuba diving equipment. He took us to the hill and bought us our passes.

"Are we ever going to sleep in the same bed twice?" I asked her on the chair lift.

"I don't know, " she said. "In fact, I don't know what's going on around me half the time. I'm worn out trying to keep up."

She did look tired.

"You're doing okay, Mom," I said. "Sheesh, I didn't know you knew so much French."

"I don't," she said. "I just nod and smile. And then I just take English words and say them with a French accent."

"What do you mean?"

"Fantastic. *Fantastique*! Marvellous? *Marveyyou*! No problem? *No ProBLAM*!"

I almost fell out of the lift.

"Anyway, tomorrow is New Year's and we'll head home after that. And … thanks, Julian."

"What for?"

"For coming. For being so great."

"Yeah. Well, the food's good."

"Still, there are so many people!"

"And he says there'll be even more tomorrow."

"*Fantastique*!" she said. And sighed.

There were seventy-two people, including Mom and me.

"We rent the whole lodge so everyone can fit," Jean-Paul told us.

"Crazy," I said. "*Crrrrazee*!" I repeated, rolling my *r*s.

It was too. Everyone was hugging. All those *bonjours*. The names all sounded the same to me. Double names. Marie-Claude. Marie-Luc. Marie-Jean. Jean-Marc. Too many to remember.

Except for one.

Bernadette.

She was about my age. She had straight black hair longer than Alanis Morisette's. Some of it covered her left eye. Her eyes were the color of forget-me-nots, and those lips. Asking for a kiss. I kept catching her looking at me, out from under her bangs.

So there we were. Seventy-two of us, sitting around the main room of the lodge.

"Have you ever seen so much food?" asked Mom.

"Or so many babies," I added as another one shot me dead. I fell to the ground and the little bugger stomped on my head.

"Show time," announced Jean-Paul.

The guitars were brought out. Everyone sang. Not just French songs, either.

"Welcome to de Otel Callyfornia," they sang. "What a lovely face," I sang. Looking right at Bernadette.

Two guys did a two-man skit. Or, rather, a two-woman skit. It was a blast, even if I didn't understand. Then we played some sort of guessing game. Well, they did. And then?

Enter Stage Left … Molly the Clown!

Chapter Ten

My mother's got some nerve. There she was, meeting all his family for the first time and what did she do? She put on her clown suit and painted her face. And did a one-woman show. I grabbed the camcorder.

Roll camera! Take One:

Bonjour, says the first card she holds up. No one says a thing. So she leans forward. She points at the card again and cups her hand over her ear. They get it.

"*Bonjour*," they all say back.

Je suis Molly, says the next card.

Je suis une anglophone, says the third. Then a fast fourth, *MAIS* ...

A fifth: *Parfois, la langue n'est pas le problem*!

There's a lot of giggling and some polite claps. Then she grabs Jean-Paul and makes him sit in a chair. He doesn't know what's going on. For ten minutes my mother, with almost no words, tells the story of how they met and fell in love. "Vroom, vroom," and "Oh là là" are the only sounds she makes. When she says, "Oh là là" she wiggles her butt, which is stuffed with pillows. And honks her red nose. And does a little hop.

She's a hit. They clap and pat Jean-Paul on the back.

She comes over to me and let's me honk her nose. Well, all you see is my hand of course. She blows kisses at the lens. Crosses her eyes. Fade to black.

Both my parents are clowns.

About nine o'clock the guys played broomball

on the ice in the field out back of the lodge. I got two goals and a good body check from Jean-Paul. I gave him a good one right back. Everyone cheered.

When I got back in, Bernadette came over to me

"You want to play?"

That's what she said. Honest to God. I stood there like an idiot. Then she repeated the question.

"You want to play card with us?" Only she said hus. Like Jean-Paul does. It's sexy when she says it.

"You speak English?" I finally spit out.

"If you speak not too fas'."

"What's the game?"

She turned and whispered something to Jean-Paul. She giggled with her hand over her mouth.

"Asshole," he said.

"What?"

"That's the name of the game, Julian. In French, it's called *Trodaycue*." That's how he said it. "You must know how to play that, Julian."

Ouch.

"Funny. Well. I don't. Troo-de-cue?" I repeated. Bernadette nodded.

"I teach you."

Jean-Paul handed me a beer halfway through the game. Mom tried to protest.

"He's in Quebec," I heard him tell her. "It's a party."

I realized all the other kids my age were sipping beer too. This province *is* distinct. Like when would this ever happen at home?

I took the beer and drank it like this was something I did every day. I can't say I liked the taste. The game didn't end, really, but we stopped to count down the New Year.

Backwards and in French. *Dix, neuf, huit*—it was a challenge. "*Bone année! Bonne année!* " Everyone started to go around kissing each other. Before I knew it, Bernadette was there in front of me. I started to just peck her on the cheek.

"No, you mus' do it the French way." I thought I'd die.

She meant on both cheeks, not a French kiss. Darn it.

It took at least half an hour to get around that room kissing everyone on both cheeks. By that time I was warmed up. I wanted to find Bernadette and give her another one. Mom found me first. She squeezed me so hard her new earrings made a dent in my face.

"They're going to pray," whispered Mom.

Jean-Paul pulled me down beside him. He held one hand. Bernadette had my other. It was something. Seventy-two people all on their knees, holding hands around a circle.

Jean-Paul's parents were in the middle.

His father was in a wheelchair. He was ancient and he spoke very slowly. Everyone was crying quiet tears. I saw one run down and drip right off Bernadette's chin. They all crossed themselves when it was over. I tried to do that like it was something I did every day too.

We ate again! A feast, this time! I was feeling a bit dizzy from the beer and so much sugar pie so I went to our room to lay down for a bit. I was supposed to sleep on the top bunk. Mom and Jean-Paul were going to be on the bottom. Real cozy, I was thinking. Then I saw them.

They were outside, on a path near the woods. The moonlight was shining right down on them. I suppose I should've looked away. But I couldn't. Instead, I got out my camcorder. He was holding her face with his hands. And planting these little quick kisses on her mouth, her nose, her chin, and her forehead. Kind kisses. Sugar kisses. Then he just looked at her. And looked at her. I mean, how long can you look at someone's face that close up without going cross-eyed? Then he wrapped his arms around her and they sort of just rocked from side to side like a rocking chair. For the longest time.

That's when it crept into my mind, sideways, when I wasn't on guard. The thought. Jean-Paul was going to be around for a while. That maybe he wouldn't be like all the others.

Chapter Eleven

Later, I went out for a walk with Bernadette. I didn't kiss her but she took my hand. I swear I could feel how warm it was through her gloves. We didn't talk much. We looked up at the moon. You don't need language when you're on the moon.

The next day as we were leaving, my mother turned and said—to everyone —"*J'aime Jean-Paul beaucoup.*" Only she didn't get it right. Everyone started giggling and then—maybe because they'd been so polite at all her other mistakes—just roared. My mother looked hurt.

"Mom, you just told everyone you loved his nice ass."

She'd said bow-cue instead of *beau-coup*. They laughed even harder at her embarrassment. Except for Bernadette.

"Hey, you understood." She pretended to clap.

"Hey, yeah, I guess I did. Wait until I tell my French teacher how I've improved my vocabulary."

"*À la prochaine*," she said as I got in the car. I think I understood that too.

"Surprise!" said Jean-Paul. He pulled into the parking lot of the Château Frontenac. I had thought we were heading straight for home.

"We have something we have to do," was all he said. We were in our room. He pointed out the window at the long line of people along the promenade, climbing the steps, taking their places and charging down on the toboggans.

Once we got outside I was sure he would change his mind. The line-up was ridiculous. It backed up way past the Château, and it was so cold people were doing jumping jacks to try to stay warm.

Jean-Paul took pictures until he discovered the camera was frozen. We waited in line an hour and a half, inching up the line every five minutes or so. I really didn't think they'd stick it out. But they did. My mother was so cold the only things chattering were her teeth. Her eyes were watering. Jean-Paul's eyebrows were frosted with ice.

When we reached the top it was dark. The city lights seemed so far below. Above us were the Plains of Abraham. I'd studied about it all. Not that I remembered much. Wolfe was the English dude. Montcalm was the leader of the French. It was pretty bloody and there have been hard feelings ever since. But it was weird thinking about it right then, with everybody all around us smiling and laughing.

"We've got the middle lane. That's the lucky one," said Jean-Paul. It wasn't supposed to be a race but of course, it was.

"Eat my dust," said the guy next to us.

"See you next year," said the kid on the other side.

A guy wearing some kind of dead animal on his head settled us in position. Then he put his hand on the lever.

"*Bonne chance*," he said as he released the brakes to let us go.

The other two toboggans shot out ahead. We were trailing far behind. Mom was screaming. The wind was fierce. Then I swear it was like someone came from behind and gave us this push. Whatever. We sailed up to them and past. We held tight and leaned forward, leaving them far behind. It felt like we'd never stop.

"They say it's going to storm," said Mom next morning. We'd just finished eating breakfast at the buffet. We were packing to leave.

"Don't worry, *chérie*," said Jean-Paul. "I'm a good driver."

It was miserable though.

There were cars zigzagging around every turn. About an hour from home, Jean-Paul's cell phone rang. Mom answered it.

"Hello. Chris! Hi, honey! How are —what? I can't understand you—oh, oh, Jesus."

There was this sound. Like she was sucking in air ready to blow up one of her balloons. Like someone had punched her in the gut.

"Tell ... tell her we'll be there soon as we can."

She sat there, staring straight head.

"My fath—oh, Daddy!" She sobbed.

She reached for me over the seat.

"It's Poppie. Poppie's dead."

Chapter Twelve

The hours and days that followed are a blur. There are scenes that are vivid still, but most are like one of those Polaroid snapshots coming into focus.

I remember sounds. The windshield wipers rubbing against the windshield as we continued on, the squeaks keeping time with my mother's weeping. Smells. Jean-Paul's cigarettes. He lit one after another. Textures. Nana's velvety skin, her wet face against my shoulder when we finally made it to her place that night. Faces. Chris's. It was all blotchy from crying, big puffy bags underneath his eyes. I remember his arms reaching out to hug me soon as he saw me. Squeezing harder when I tried to wriggle away, until I stopped. Then I hung on to him for dear life.

I got sick in the car right after Mom told us how Poppie died. An aneurysm. Blood clot in the brain.

Jean-Paul stopped the car and got out with me. He stood beside me the whole time, in the blinding storm, while I woofed my cookies.

He kept patting my back and saying, "Let it go, Julian, let it go." I kept barfing and screaming into the wind.

He wiped my mouth with the sleeve of his coat.

The church was packed for the funeral. Everyone was there. Even Dad and Erika. Dad hugged me so hard I couldn't breathe. No thwacking or pinching. A real hug. Everyone knew how I felt about Poppie.

"You okay, Jules?" he asked into my ear.

"No," I said. "I'm not okay at all, Dad."

"Your granddad was one of the good guys," he said.

Erika was blowing her nose. "Honey, I am so sorry," was all she said before we had to go into the church.

Nana, me, Chris, Mom and Jean-Paul sat up front.

I don't remember the words. Just the songs. There were three. Two were taped and piped into the church. The other sung by a Barbershop quartet made up of some old railroad pals.

The first song was Louis Armstrong's "What a Wonderful World." Poppie's favorite of all time. He used to do a wicked imitation. Chris lost it then.

The second was called "People Get Ready." It's about a train that's going to heaven, I guess. Mom cried into Jean-Paul's shoulder.

But let me tell you, when those old guys dressed in their uniforms got up there and sang, "I've Been Working on The Railroad," there wasn't a dry eye anywhere. Except for me.

At the end of the song they played a two-minute tape recording of train whistles. I hadn't expected that. "Poppie," I whispered and that lump in my throat burst like it was some sort of dam holding back my tears. Nana squeezed my hand. I let her hold me while I bawled like some big baby. Those damn whistles.

Poppie heard.

I'm sure of it.

Chris was right as usual. I only used this diary for a bit, then forgot about it. I dug it out today because I figured I needed to add a page or two. Things change in a year and half. Things can change in a moment, for that matter.

Anyway. They did it. Tied the noose. I mean the knot. Yep. Jean-Paul and Mom got married today. In Nana and Poppie's backyard, with the garden in full bloom. It was a picture-perfect day. I kept thinking it was going to rain. I figure Poppie made sure it didn't.

Chris and I walked Mom up the garden

path to where Jean-Paul was waiting. Mom looked scared but beautiful. Her dress was this floaty, lacy thing and she had flowers tucked in her hair. Like wow! Not bad for an old bride! There were big bouquets of pink and purple balloons on either side of the patio where they said their vows. In English and French, of course. The balloons were a big hit. There were almost more kids than adults in the crowd. Almost every kid who ever went through Thumbalina's Day Care Center showed up.

Anyhow, Chris and I took part in the ceremony too. Well, all we had to say was, "I do," after some prayer about committing to this new family. I did. Say, "I do," I mean. And it was the only moment I was a smart-ass all day. I scratched my head first and said, "I dunno," then, "Oh, yeah, I do!" It got a laugh. Well, we needed a break at that point. Comic relief. They gave me and Chris rings too. Mine's too big. I'll grow into it.

Maybe when I do, I'll have grown used to Jean-Paul too. Most of the time, we get on. My French is better and so is his English.

He wants me to go scuba diving with him sometime. We'll see. I don't trust him that much yet! We had one big scene after we all moved in together last year.

One Friday night, I stayed out past my curfew. Okay, so the sun was coming up by the time I made it home. Jean-Paul was waiting. Mom was in bed. I have a feeling she heard it all.

"You're supposed to call if you're going to be late," he said. In almost perfect English.

"Sorry," I said. I just wanted to get to bed. I tiptoed past him, stumbled and knocked over a chair.

"How much have you had to drink?"

"A few beers."

"Looks like a lot of beers to me."

"Goodnight,' I said.

"See you tomorrow," he said.

I hurried to my room and prayed for the ceiling to stop spinning. Then I grinned. Well, I thought, that was easy. He never even yelled. The wuss.

At seven o'clock the next morning he pounded on my door. "Get up, Julian."

"Why? It's Saturday." I moaned.

"I need your help." He was still outside my bedroom door.

"What for?"

"I need your muscles. Have to bring the tub in the house." He was re-doing the bathroom.

"Later," I mumbled and turned over.

"I have to do it now."

"Sorry," I said.

He opened the door quietly. In a voice just as quiet he said, "It will only take ten minutes."

"Get out!" I yelled.

"Want the cold water treatment?" He was holding a pitcher of water over my head.

"You wouldn't dare."

He started to tip it. So, I huffed and threw off the covers. "Get out," I said, "I'll be right there."

"I'll be in the driveway," he smiled.

I pulled on a shirt, hauled on my sweats and stuffed my bare feet into my sneakers. I stood up. That's when it felt like someone hit me with a two-by-four. And my stomach.

It started to churn as if someone was in there trying to make butter.

That tub was a heavy monster. "Lift on three," he ordered. "*Un, deux, trois*."

I grunted and groaned and pulled. I couldn't budge my end. Then, I lost it. I don't mean my temper. I mean the contents of my stomach. I threw up in the driveway.

Jean-Paul just stood there with his arms folded. His grin was dorkier than ever. No patting me on the back this time.

"Your mother was worried sick last night," he began. "So was I. Why did you drink until you got drunk?"

"It was a p-p-party." I was still retching.

"Pretty stupid thing to do."

"Who are you calling stupid?"

"No one. I said it was a stupid thing to do. You could poison yourself and die that way."

"Why would you care?"

"Anyway, you're grounded. Not because you got pissed. You'll pay today for that. You'll suffer. Believe me. We ground you, your mother and I, for breaking curfew and not calling, for not thinking about the results."

"Who are you to tell me—you're not —"

"Your father? I know this. I never will be. But, I am going to be here, Julian. For your mother. And for you, if you need me. Always. *Toujours*."

"Always?" I was wiping the dribble from my mouth. My throat was burning, filled with bile. "I don't believe in *toujours*, okay? That's for idiots like you."

I expected anger, hollering. He started to laugh.

"Who looks like the idiot at this moment?" I looked down at myself. Gross. "Go back to bed and sleep it off. I'll get a neighbor to help me with this ... monster tub. And ... don't go near your mother yet. She's ready to ..." He drew his finger across his throat, "you know, make you suffer more."

I was sick all day. He brought me in toast and tea after supper. "Eat slowly," he said. "When you're ready, go tell your mother you are sorry." Oh, was I sorry.

The wedding reception was a huge party and dance. All J.P's family was there (yeah he's J.P. to me now)—including Bernadette. Sweet Bernadette. I boogied the night away with sweet Bernadette. I even got a real French kiss before the night was through. Maybe two. Maybe three.

Don't go there.

Tomorrow, Chris has to leave for his summer job out west. He was away at school all this last year and I hate to admit it, but I missed him loads. Even the look.

I'm glad for him though.

"I spent the year being bad," he keeps telling me. He won't give details. Probably finally kissed Becca or used a condom.

So, I'm off to spend a week with Dad and Erika and the Munsters. We're camping in the valley. Should be cool. Since J.P.'s been around, it seems Dad has made more time for me. Or maybe, I've made more time for him.

Until the lovebirds come home from their honeymoon, I'll be here with Nana. She's so lonesome without Poppie, it breaks my heart.

"Julian, you're so like him," she keeps telling me. "Stubborn and bow-legged and immature for your age." Now, that, I take as a compliment. When I am at their place, I think Poppie's still around. I half expect him to come up behind me and put me in a headlock and shout, "Say Uncle!" I go to the basement and fool around with his electric train set. He left it to me. It came with a note. Nana says he wrote the note years ago when he thought he had cancer. "To Julian. Remember, Poppie loves ya. And son, all us men realize sooner or later, we must learn to be fathers to ourselves." I think a lot on that. I've had a lot of role models to pick from.

I don't know what's ahead for us as a family, really. I showed them edited videotape of our trip to Quebec last night. With music and everything. They loved it. Especially what I called "The Lovebirds in Moonlight or Caught Ya!" Even got a high-speed shot traveling down that toboggan hill. Seems like a long time ago now.

"In good times and hard times," they said in their vows to each other. Instead of "for better or worse." I guess they know, at their age, there's no real happy ever after. There's just … after. But that's something. It's really something. Maybe it's everything.

More Orca Soundings

My Time as Caz Hazard
by Tanya Lloyd Kyi

"How can you be like this? What if this was our fault?" I could feel my voice growing loud and shrill.

"Shut up!" Amanda grabbed my arm, hard. "You're not making sense. What did we have to do with it? No one kills herself over a ripped shirt. Understand?"

Moving to a new school, Caz is told she is dyslexic and sent to Special Education classes. She tries to fit in and get by while suffering the taunts and abuse that others throw at the students in her class. Her friendship with Amanda leads her into new territory—shoplifting and skipping school. Coupled with her parents' impending separation, her life is anything but stable and continues to spiral out of control. And when Caz and Amanda's behavior seems to contribute to a classmate's suicide, Caz must take a long hard look at her life.

More Orca Soundings

Charmed
by Carrie Mac

Cody Dillon comes and rescues me (RESCUES ME!). He takes me to his apartment (HIS OWN APARTMENT!) and runs me a bubble bath. He lights a bunch of candles and turns the light off. He sits on the floor and keeps me company. He says I can stay here as long as I want. Um, hello, heaven? Izzy McAfferty has arrived, in case anyone wants to know.

Izzy's mother works far away and leaves Izzy at home, alone with Rob the Slob. Angry at her mother and trying to deal with school, friends and the attentions of charismatic Cody Dillon, Izzy finds her life swirling out of control. After "borrowing" money from her mother's boyfriend, she is forced to leave home until she can repay it. Ending up with Cody and living in the city, Izzy makes misguided choices that are all wrong.

TITLES IN THE
ORCA SOUNDINGS SERIES